SCHOOL
DAYS
RECORD
BOOK

◆ ✧ ◆

Illustrated by Helen Cann

BLITZ EDITIONS

ALL ABOUT ME

◇ ◇

My name is

_____

I began this record on

_____

I was born on

_____

My mother's full name

_____

Her job is

_____

My father's name is

_____

His job is

_____

My grandparents and their jobs

_____

_____

_____

_____

My brothers and sisters

_____

_____

_____

_____

Our pets

_____

_____

We live at

Date we moved here

◇ Family photograph ◇

Nursery School

◇ ✦ ◇

Name of school

_____

Dates attended

_____

Name of teacher

_____

What I thought of my teacher

_____

What she thought of me

_____

Our activities included

_____

_____

_____

My favourite activity was

_____

At break time, we were given

_____

My best friends were

_____

_____

_____

_____

Our school trip was to

_____

_____

At the Christmas party we

_____

_____

_____

_____

Our school play was

_____

_____

I took part as

_____

_____

⬥ School photograph ⬥

At the end of the year, I could:

count up to

_____

say the alphabet up to

_____

recognise these letters

_____

When I grow up, I would like to be

_____

_____

_____

_____

◇ Sample of my handwriting ◇

◇ My self portrait ◇

Height   Weight   Shoe size

RECEPTION

◇ ◇ ◇

Name of school

_____

Name of class and dates attended

_____

Name of teacher

_____

What I thought of my teacher

_____

What she thought of me

_____

I was picked up from school by

_____

What I wore to school

_____

Favourite subjects

_____

Favourite sports

_____

What I ate during the day

_____

My best friends were

_____

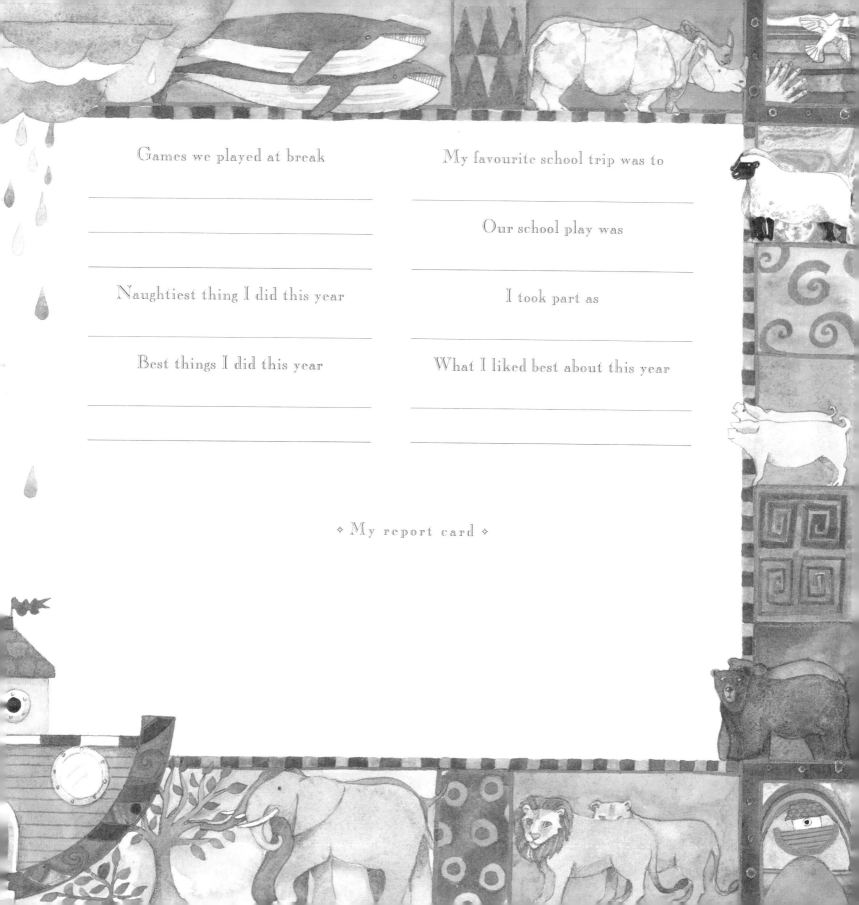

Games we played at break

_____

_____

_____

Naughtiest thing I did this year

_____

Best things I did this year

_____

_____

My favourite school trip was to

_____

Our school play was

_____

I took part as

_____

What I liked best about this year

_____

_____

◇ My report card ◇

Clubs I joined

New skills I acquired

Special projects

When I grow up, I would like to be

Special memories of this year

◇ School photograph ◇

How I have changed

◇ ✧ ◇

◇ My self portrait ◇

Height   Weight   Shoe size

My First Year

◇ ◇ ◇

Name of school

_____

Name of class and dates attended

_____

Name of teacher

_____

What I thought of my teacher

_____

What she thought of me

_____

I was picked up from school by

_____

What I wore to school

_____

Favourite subjects

_____

_____

Favourite sports

_____

What I ate during the day

_____

My best friends were

_____

_____

_____

Games we played at break

_____

_____

_____

Naughtiest thing I did this year

_____

Best things I did this year

_____

_____

My favourite school trip was to

_____

Our school play was

_____

I took part as

_____

What I liked best about this year

_____

_____

◇ My report card ◇

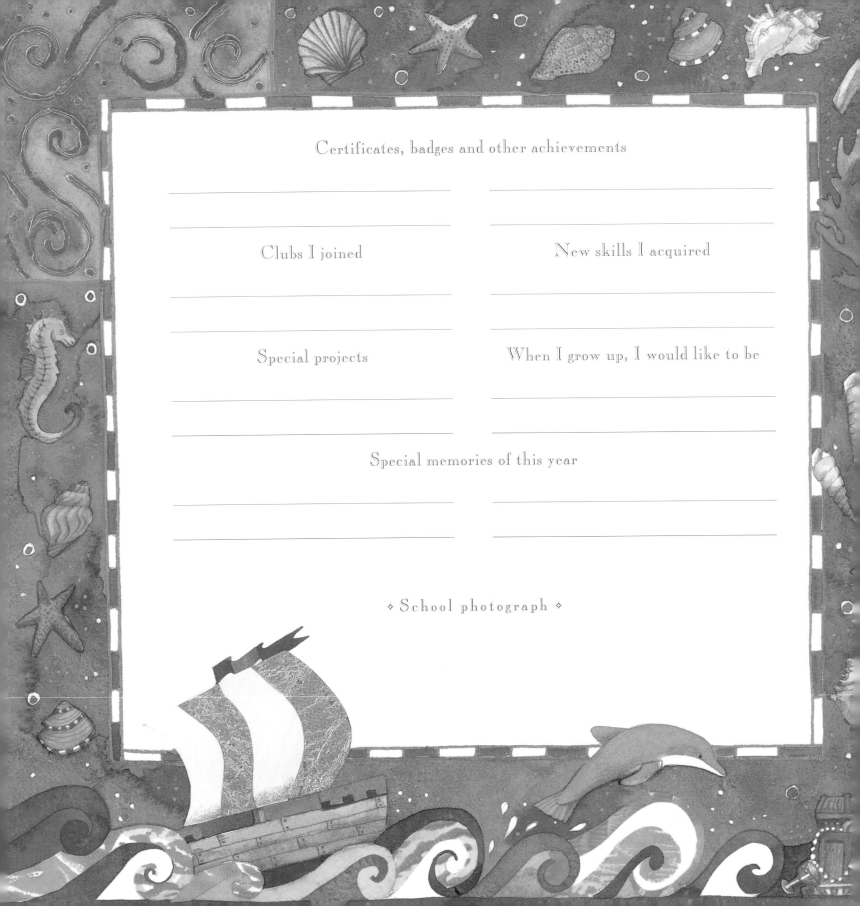

Certificates, badges and other achievements

_____

_____

Clubs I joined

New skills I acquired

_____

_____

Special projects

When I grow up, I would like to be

_____

_____

Special memories of this year

_____

_____

◇ School photograph ◇

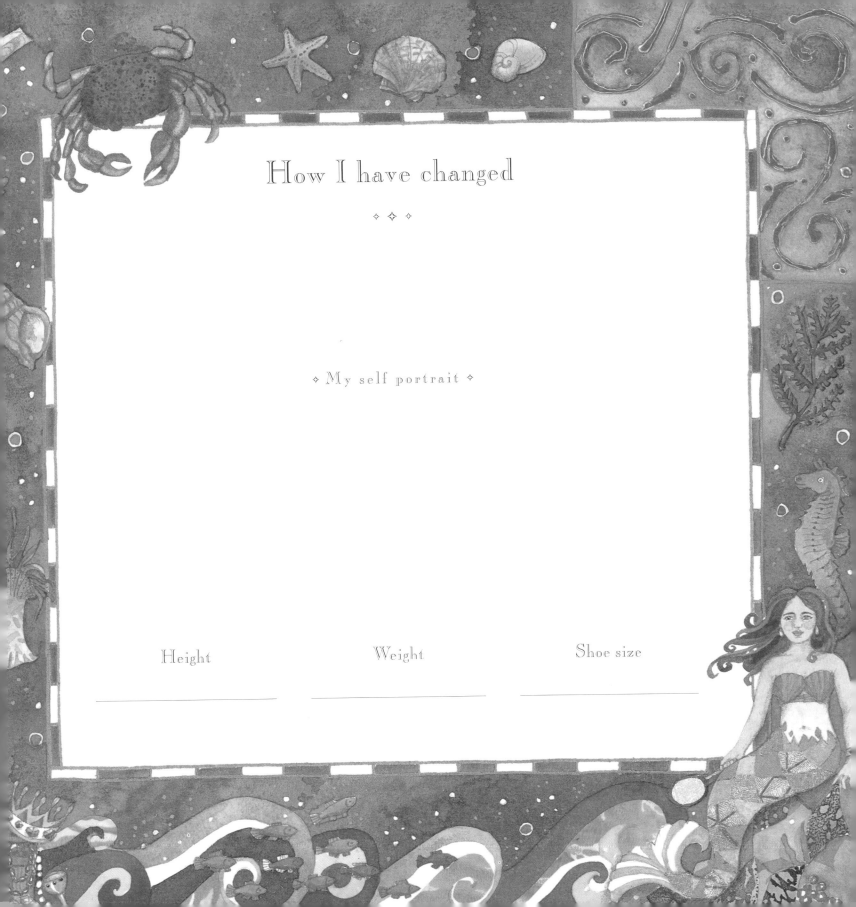

How I have changed

◇ ✦ ◇

✧ My self portrait ✧

Height   Weight   Shoe size

My Second Year

◇ ✦ ◇

Name of school

_____

Name of class and dates attended

_____

Name of teacher

_____

What I thought of my teacher

_____

What she thought of me

_____

I was picked up from school by

_____

What I wore to school

_____

Favourite subjects

_____

_____

Favourite sports

_____

_____

What I ate during the day

_____

My best friends were

_____

_____

Games we played at break

_____

_____

_____

Naughtiest thing I did this year

_____

Best things I did this year

_____

_____

My favourite school trip was to

_____

Our school play was

_____

I took part as

_____

What I liked best about this year

_____

_____

◇ My report card ◇

Certificates, badges and other achievements

_____

Clubs I joined

New skills I acquired

Special projects

When I grow up, I would like to be

Special memories of this year

⋄ School photograph ⋄

How I have changed

◇ ✧ ◇

◇ My self portrait ◇

Height

Weight

Shoe size

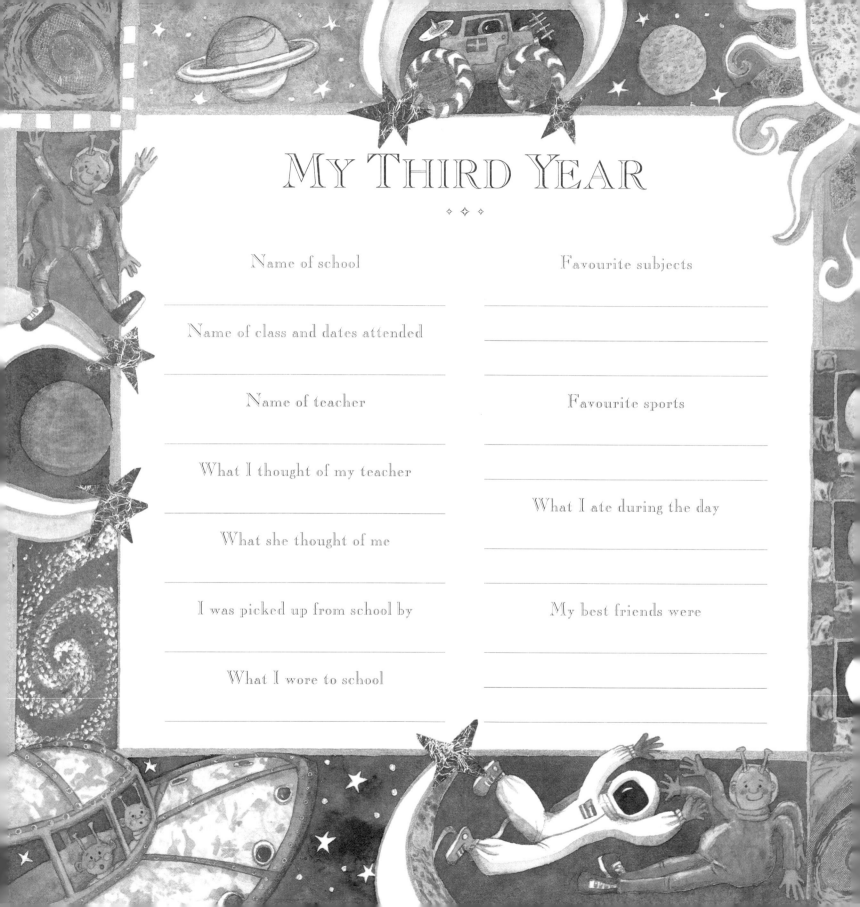

MY THIRD YEAR

◇ ◈ ◇

Name of school

Name of class and dates attended

Name of teacher

What I thought of my teacher

What she thought of me

I was picked up from school by

What I wore to school

Favourite subjects

Favourite sports

What I ate during the day

My best friends were

Games we played at break

_____

_____

Naughtiest thing I did this year

_____

Best things I did this year

_____

_____

My favourite school trip was to

_____

Our school play was

_____

I took part as

_____

What I liked best about this year

_____

◊ My report card ◊

Certificates, badges and other achievements

_____

Clubs I joined   New skills I acquired

_____

Special projects   When I grow up, I would like to be

_____

Special memories of this year

_____

⋄ School photograph ⋄

How I have changed

◇ ✧ ◇

✧ My self portrait ✧

Height　　　　　　　　　Weight　　　　　　　　　Shoe size

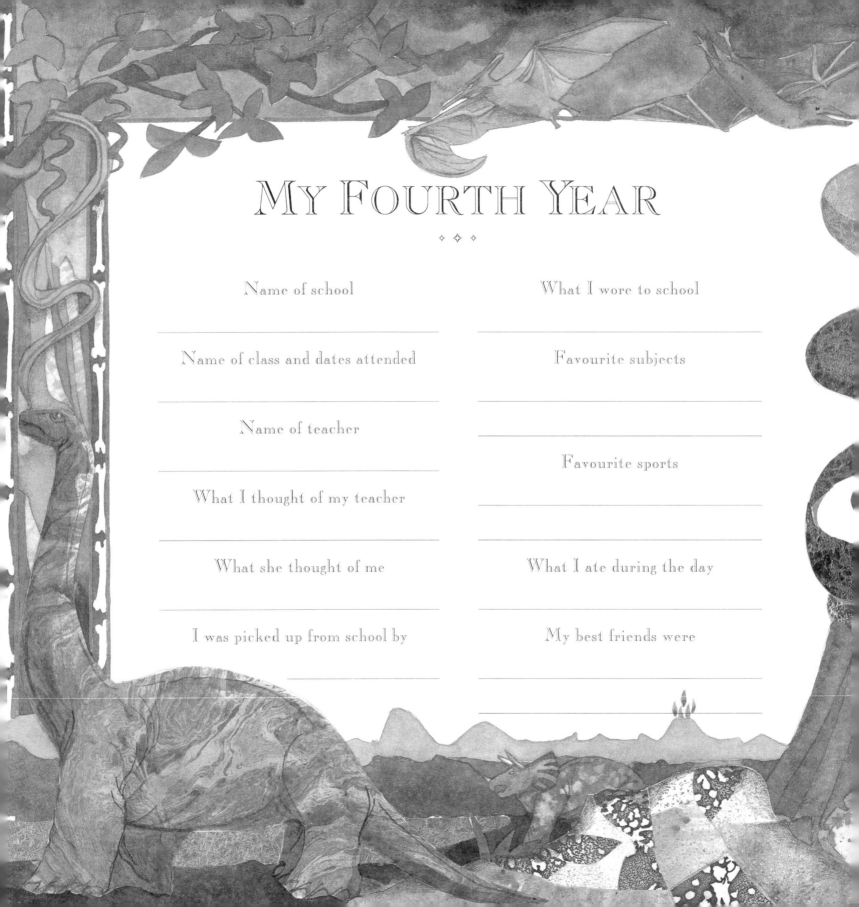

MY FOURTH YEAR

⋄ ✧ ⋄

Name of school

_____

Name of class and dates attended

_____

Name of teacher

_____

What I thought of my teacher

_____

What she thought of me

_____

I was picked up from school by

_____

What I wore to school

_____

Favourite subjects

_____

Favourite sports

_____

What I ate during the day

_____

My best friends were

_____

_____

Games we played at break

My favourite school trip was to

Our school play was

Naughtiest thing I did this year

I took part as

Best things I did this year

What I liked best about this year

◇ My report card ◇

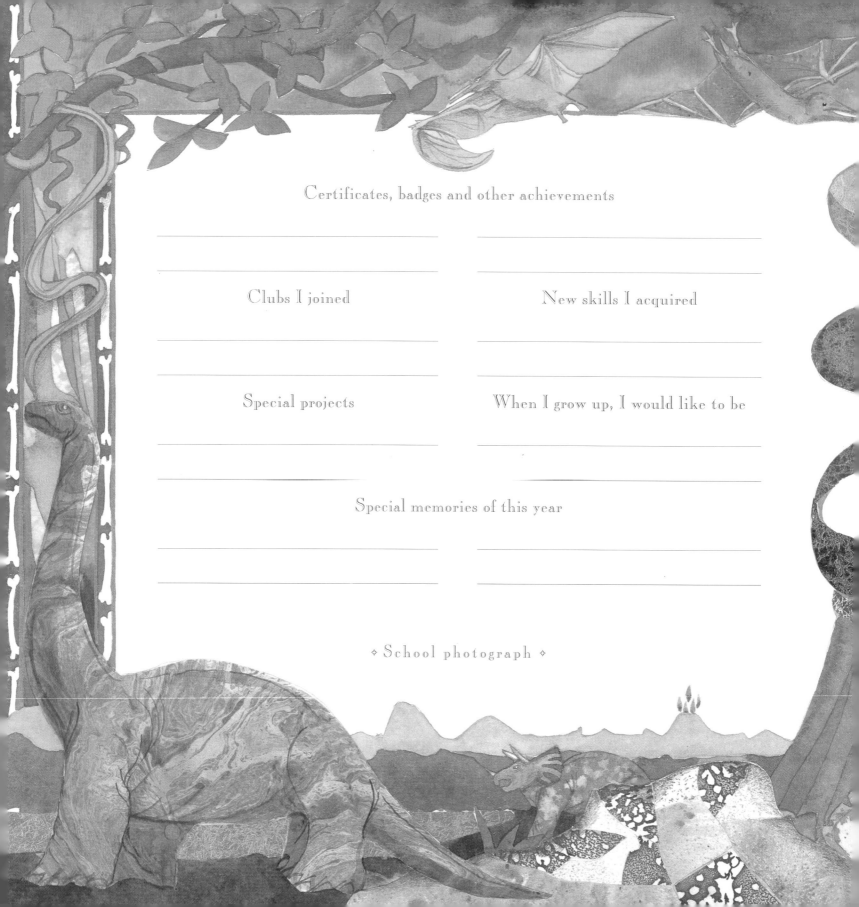

Certificates, badges and other achievements

_____

_____

Clubs I joined

New skills I acquired

_____

_____

Special projects

When I grow up, I would like to be

_____

_____

Special memories of this year

_____

_____

◇ School photograph ◇

How I have changed

⋄ ◇ ⋄

⋄ My self portrait ⋄

Height   Weight   Shoe size

MY FIFTH YEAR

◇ ✧ ◇

Name of school

_____

Name of class and dates attended

_____

Name of teacher

_____

What I thought of my teacher

_____

What she thought of me

_____

I was picked up from school by

_____

What I wore to school

_____

Favourite subjects

_____

_____

Favourite sports

_____

_____

What I ate during the day

_____

_____

My best friends were

_____

_____

Games we played at break

_____

_____

_____

Naughtiest thing I did this year

_____

Best things I did this year

_____

_____

My favourite school trip was to

_____

Our school play was

_____

I took part as

_____

What I liked best about this year

_____

_____

◇ My report card ◇

Certificates, badges and other achievements

_____

_____

Clubs I joined

New skills I acquired

_____

_____

Special projects

When I grow up, I would like to be

_____

_____

Special memories of this year

_____

_____

◇ School photograph ◇

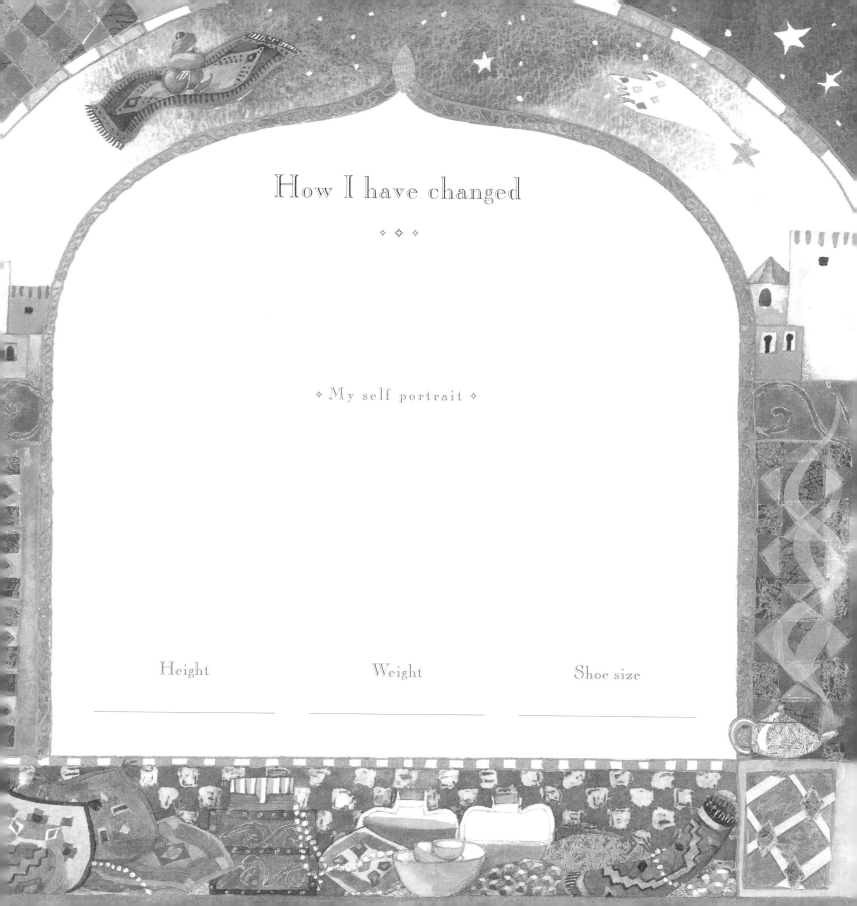

How I have changed

◇ ✧ ◇

◇ My self portrait ◇

Height	Weight	Shoe size

My Sixth Year

◇ ◇ ◇

Name of school

Favourite subjects

Name of class and dates attended

Name of teacher

Favourite sports

What I thought of my teacher

What I ate during the day

What she thought of me

I was picked up from school by

My best friends were

What I wore to school

Games we played at break

_____

_____

_____

Naughtiest thing I did this year

_____

Best things I did this year

_____

_____

My favourite school trip was to

_____

Our school play was

_____

I took part as

_____

What I liked best about this year

_____

_____

◇ My report card ◇

Certificates, badges and other achievements

_____   _____

_____   _____

Clubs I joined   New skills I acquired this year

_____   _____

_____   _____

Special projects   When I grow up, I would like to be

_____   _____

_____   _____

Special memories of this year

_____   _____

_____   _____

⋄ School photograph ⋄

How I have changed

◇ ✧ ◇

◇ My self portrait ◇

Height   Weight   Shoe size

MY SEVENTH YEAR

Name of school

_____

Name of class and dates attended

_____

How I travelled to school

_____

Names of favourite teachers

_____

_____

Favourite subjects

_____

_____

_____

Favourite sports

_____

_____

For our school trips we went to

_____

_____

My best friends were

_____

_____

_____

What we did during the lunch hour

_____

_____

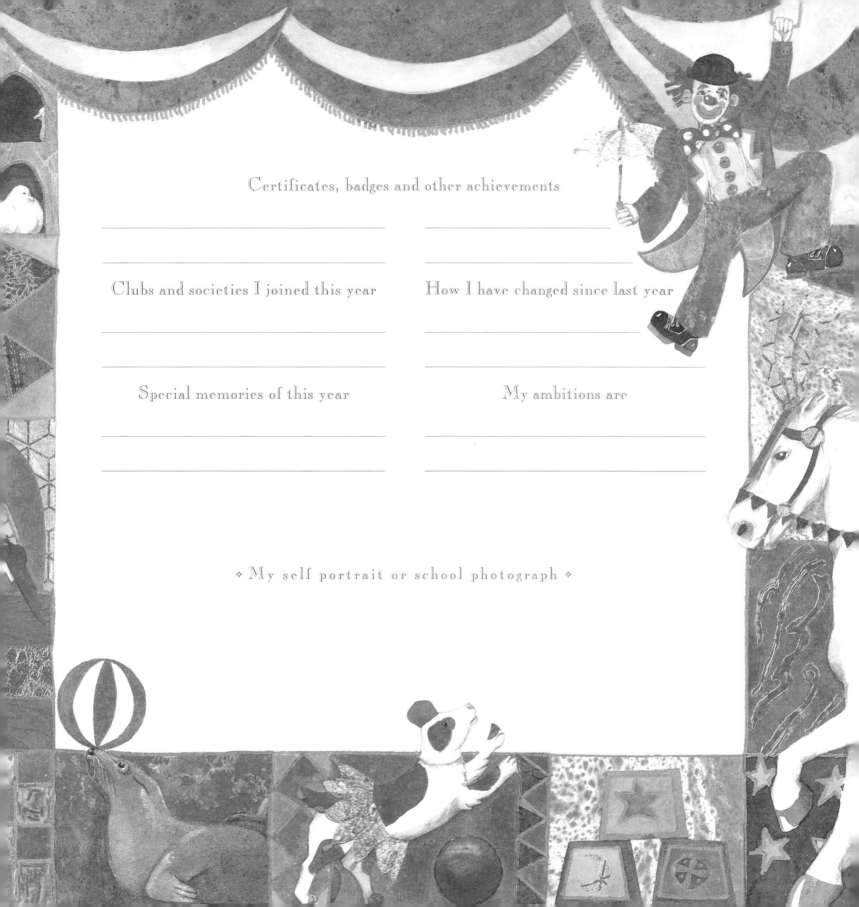

Certificates, badges and other achievements

_____   _____

_____   _____

Clubs and societies I joined this year   How I have changed since last year

_____   _____

_____   _____

Special memories of this year   My ambitions are

_____   _____

_____   _____

⋄ My self portrait or school photograph ⋄

My Eighth Year

⋄ ✧ ⋄

Name of school

_____

Name of class and dates attended

_____

How I travelled to school

_____

Names of favourite teachers

_____

_____

Favourite subjects

_____

_____

Favourite sports

_____

For our school trips we went to

_____

_____

My best friends were

_____

_____

_____

What we did during the lunch hour

_____

_____

Certificates, badges and other achievements

_____

_____

Clubs and societies I joined this year

_____

Special memories of this year

_____

How I have changed since last year

_____

My ambitions are

_____

⬥ My self portrait or school photograph ⬥

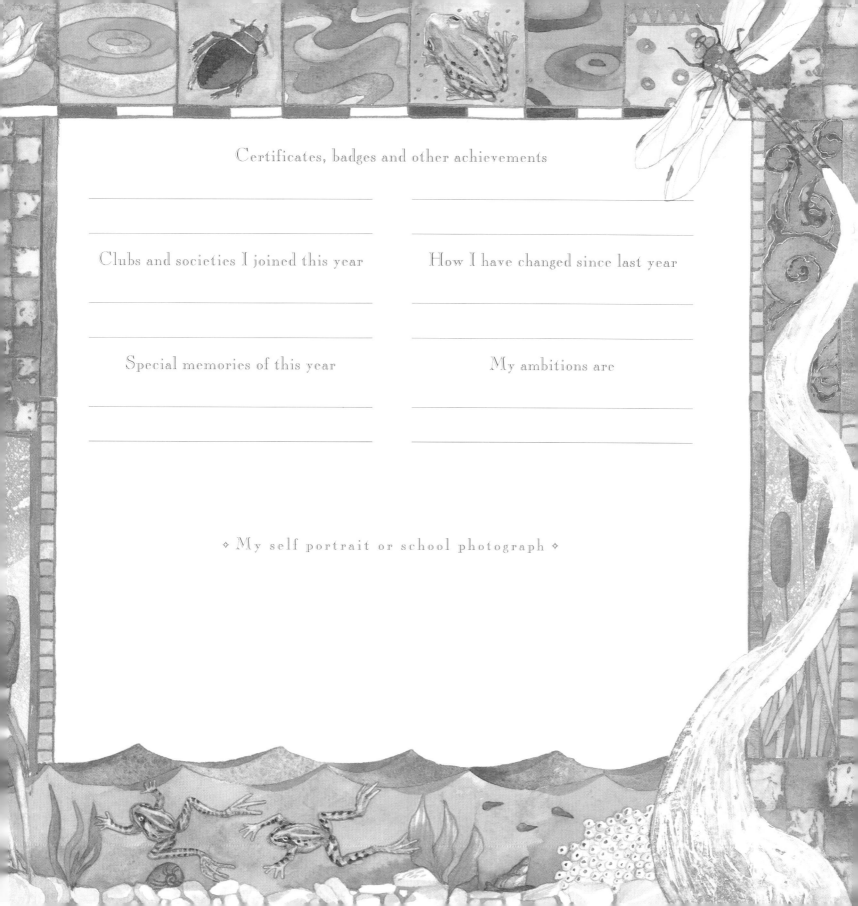

My Ninth Year

◇ ✧ ◇

Name of school

_____

Name of class and dates attended

_____

How I travelled to school

_____

Names of favourite teachers

_____

_____

Favourite subjects

_____

_____

_____

Favourite sports

_____

_____

For our school trips we went to

_____

_____

My best friends were

_____

_____

_____

What we did during the lunch hour

_____

_____

Certificates, badges and other achievements

_____   _____

_____   _____

Clubs and societies I joined this year   How I have changed since last year

_____   _____

_____   _____

Special memories of this year   My ambitions are

_____   _____

_____   _____

◇ My self portrait or school photograph ◇

MY TENTH YEAR

◇ ✧ ◇

Name of school

_____

Name of class and dates attended

_____

How I travelled to school

_____

Names of favourite teachers

_____

_____

Favourite subjects

_____

_____

Favourite sports

_____

_____

For our school trips we went to

_____

My best friends were

_____

_____

_____

What we did during the lunch hour

_____

_____

Certificates, badges and other achievements

_____

_____

Clubs and societies I joined this year

How I have changed since last year

_____

_____

Special memories of this year

My ambitions are

_____

_____

◇ My self portrait or school photograph ◇

MY ELEVENTH YEAR

❖ ◇ ❖

Name of school

_____

Name of class and dates attended

_____

How I travelled to school

_____

Names of favourite teachers

_____

_____

Favourite subjects

_____

_____

_____

Favourite sports

_____

_____

For our school trips we went to

_____

_____

My best friends were

_____

_____

_____

_____

What we did during the lunch hour

_____

_____

Certificates, badges and other achievements

_____

_____

Clubs and societies I joined this year

How I have changed since last year

Special memories of this year

My ambitions are

✧ My self portrait or school photograph ✧

MY PLANS FOR THE FUTURE

✦ ✦ ✦

Now you have reached the age when you start to make your own decisions. There are so many options – to stay on at school full-time, to take a year off and go abroad, to study part-time or at evening classes, to specialise in a vocational training, or to leave the world of education behind you altogether. Whatever you choose, write down your plans here so that you can enjoy reading them later in life.

Further education plans

_____

_____

_____

_____

Career plans

_____

_____

_____

_____

Working holiday plans

_____

_____

_____

Travel plans

_____

_____

_____

Family plans

_____

_____

_____

_____

Dreams and ambitions

_____

_____

_____

_____

A Record of my Exam Results

◇ ◇ ◇

Subject	Date taken	Results

◇ Paste your exam certificates here ◇